Library of Congress Catalog Card Number
2005908144

ISBN 1598721208

First Printing October 2005

Front cover and layout by
Jeff MacKinder

Dedication

To Ed Letts, he told me to write a book.

Contents

The rhythm of the waterfall, music
Little angels dancing on the floor
They should be dancing on the clouds
Here I am
The music playing on my head
Dreams, thoughts of another life
Looking in obscurity lit by speed
Here I am
I grab her and start to dance
Rhythm inside my blood
Movements, steps, and turns
Smelling the abundance of her hair
Here I am
I am flying in a foreign country
The music, women, and liquid
All this tropical, exotic, something different
Drinking it all I am living
Never will forget, I was here

Paisano's Passion

Rent

Why? That is the question I ask myself day after day as the summer wears on. Why go to Mexico? Why escape my family plans? Why seek gainful employment right away? Why spend time away from the United States? Why learn Spanish? Why do I find Latina women so exciting? Why follow my instinct?

I'll answer why eventually, but for now I need to sleep so I can get up at 5:00 a.m. and ride my bike to work. Luna, my girlfriend is sprawled out next to me, in a deep sleep. I don't want to wake her up, but she has all the covers squished up underneath her curvy figure. I inhale her sweet strawberry shampoo and drift into coverless dreams.

The alarm shrieks and rocks me upright to turn it off. My head aches from the five hours of sleep while my brain cells whisper to lie for just another seven minutes. I know better than to listen to this whiney invitation. When I over sleep my boss docks 10% of my commissions. I scratch my chest and maneuver my feet to the side of the bed. Inhaling deeply and rubbing the sleep from my eyes I stumble into the shower. The hot water jumping on my body wakes me up. I get dressed and tip-toe to the bed. Again her Salon Selectives enter my nose. Her lovely bouquet invites a peck on the forehead.

"Baby go to work, you are making too much noise," Not exactly the encouragement I want at 5:15 in the morning. I shrug my shoulders letting out a quick breath and head out the door.

Cool morning air of Isla Vista shimmies through my thin jacket. The quick speed of the bike sends the chill in even deeper.

"No law school, no financial help. You want to live with your girlfriend, fine, you can drive her around on your bike, not my car." The voice of my father rings in my ears with the downhill wind every morning.

I lock my ten-speed to the Bargain Property bike rack. My parents only want the best for me, but I'll make my own way. I slam the silver metal bar that opens the door and enter the building.

Stale walls and hurrying stress slap my face while walking down the hallway to my cubicle. Collapsing into the cubicle with a thin film of sweat on my brow, the backpack knocks into my chair.

A co-worker manipulates a customer on the telephone line, "I will send that out to you for a trial month you can return it anytime with no further obligation. "

After he explains that the car auction information will arrive by mail, my co-worker commands the customer to give out the Visa card number. Telemarketers avoid asking too many questions; the secret relies on making sales with the attitude of a college registration clerk. The customer has one option, buy. Keeping his voice down, my cubicle companion tries to persuade the card holder with authority.

"Are you going to use Visa, Mastercard, American Express or Discover?" He asks a question, but it sounds like a statement.

The customer answers, "I have a Visa card."

"The number on your card starts with a four, go ahead." My associate's face goes blank, then flashes into a scowl as he pounds the new call button on the phone. "Shit, another burned call!" he mutters in disgust.

I try to keep a positive attitude, but the smell, dingy red cubicle, and my scowling neighbor push my head into my hands. What was I thinking when I took a job as a telemarketer? Slamming my headphones down I repeat to myself, "Here comes Mexico, here comes Mexico." This is the chant I use to sell the most car auction packets I can sell. The sales coach pitches these psychological tricks to all the sales representatives during our eight-hour training. Being an idealistic college graduate, I buy into this Amway type motivation and chant away. My mantra, and the reasons why I am here are interrelated: girlfriend, and some day Mexico.

"Bargain Network, your extension number. That's R125 and your area code, that's 93456." I keep my voice deep and baritone to imitate a man of confidence. The pace is brisk to let the customer know I'm doing them a favor and it would serve them well to listen up and buy.

"Do you have any double wides?" A caller twangs. I get a considerable amount of white trash calling daily. We're intertwined in a salesman's web, struggling to resolve who feeds on green bills. "I want to buy one of those double wides I saw on the TV."

"Yes we have double wides, I'll get that information out to you for a trial month." I actually wasn't sure we had information on double wide mobile homes. This line of work was making me into a liar. I figured he could look up the information once he got the company's information packet. With one purchase, plus complementary coupons and a phone card, I could make $8 per sale, but the secret is to convince the customer to sign up for all three services with the shipping and handling fee of $9.95. In one day, I can make 20 sales and bring home $160.

"No I'm not interested, thank you much." Click.

Next call, next call, next call. After six hours my supervisor comes over. "Two for sixty five Anthony, go home. You burned sixty three calls, today is not your day," he advises.

"Just let me try another hour, I'll get it right" I plead.

"All right. Half an hour. If you don't sell by then get out of here." The big boss speaks. Bargain Property, Bargain Property, Bargain Property... No sales. I whip off my headphones, gather up my sales scripts, and stuff them into my backpack. Out of my cubicle, I walk down the carpeted hallway to the door. A nod to the floor supervisor and that's my sales day. Pushing open the doors, I stomp over to the bike rack and unlock my ride.

This is my only chance for making money. There's no time to get another job and I have to pay July's rent. I'm $500 in the hole to my uncle, who was cool enough to loan me the money for June, making the transition from student to worker. His pay back is due July first, the same day as the rent, and it is important to me to be punctual with my family, no extensions. I chant to myself, "Here comes Mexico," over and over again and pedal back to my apartment.

Legs achy from standing in the cubicle to stay awake, attempting to sell to stupid customers, and after a half an hour bike ride, I collapse onto the bed. The pillow perfumed by her curly hair lulls me to sleep as I float on the soft covers. My eyelids get heavier and heavier, darkness.

Cars hum outside my window and the yellow lights of the lamp posts filter through the half open blinds. Crashing pots and pans of our roommates in the kitchen wake me up. Refreshed from my afternoon power nap I gulp down the glass of water at my bedside, washing out the gym sock flavor on my dry tongue. I haven't gone for my daily run yet; and my muscles, despite being sleep deprived, are cranky for a dose of endorphins. Luna slides through my bedroom door. "What are you doing in bed? Tony, you haven't even fixed dinner yet." She complains.

I say, defensively, "I was tired from work and took a nap. I'm feeling anxious, I need to go for a run."

Luna mimics, "I need to go for a run."

"Fix your own dinner, I'm going for a run." I'm getting hot now.

She argues, "Always running, what about me? Last night you said you'd make dinner. I was in school all day."

"Great, another argument," I blow under my breath. I leave the room and head for the apartment door, leaving Luna to herself. Thoughts whirl in my mind, if I pay all the rent why do I have to make her dinner too.

Exploding out the front door, my shoes make a familiar pressing sound on the black pavement. After just half a mile my breathing is heavy and sweat sticks to the back of my T-shirt. Warm California air caresses my arms and I feel the blood pounding through my veins delivering tiny bubbles of energy to my tired legs and arms. By the end of the fourth mile my body is on fire with endorphins. I stop to stretch my muscles smooth into long lines and runner's high sets in. Now I can deal with her monthly mood.

The kitchen is dark and the roommates' pots are put away. I squeak open the door. Luna is lying on the bed. I can feel her anger throughout the dark room. "Shut the door Tony, you're letting in the living room light," she snaps.

"Why didn't you fix yourself something to eat?" I ask.

"I didn't want to, I'm not hungry now. You know what? You only think about yourself and you never listen to me," she lectures.

"Wait a minute," I disagree. "Last night I stayed up 'til midnight listening to problems with your sister and your city college classes."

"Baby, please fix me a sandwich and bring me a scoop of ice cream. I'll give you dessert later tonight." She purrs. With a mild grin, I roll back my eyes, open the door and march into the kitchen. I lay out the tuna fish, lettuce, and tomatoes onto toasted wheat bread. Taking a sharp knife I cut the sandwich into triangles the way she likes it. One scoop of mint chocolate chip ice cream falls into the glass bowl from the pint of Dreyer's. I creep into the room. She's sitting up on the corner of the bed with the lights on.

She giggles, "You are the best boyfriend," and snatches the food from my hands.

Watching her munch on tuna and spooning down mint green cream, I don't feel like food. I slip into the shower to wash off the run's sweat. When I get out of the shower and towel off, she finishes up her meal and places the plate and bowl at the side of the bed. I see her eye my sleek runner's frame. She pulls the towel down from my waist, "Come here big boy," she whispers. As I slip into her tanned arms and red lips I think of the hours left alone in a cubicle and the tempting pull of southern guitars.

Three months of tenacity pays off. I have more than enough money to start off at a Spanish school in Cuernavaca. More of Luna's demands and intoxicating suggestions have clouded my mind. The pull of another life becomes a tug of war inside my gut.

"When you get back from Mexico, you need to make more of a commitment to me. I want to be married within the year." Her words ring in my head, as she searches for some grounding on which to steady her own life. Eyes narrowing, her voice becomes serious. "Tony are you listening? I need a promise, something to hold onto."

"You don't understand what I've gone through this summer." I say, shaking my head. I try to get her to see the picture clearly. "I love you, Luna. I respect your plans, but I won't make the decision you want now. This is my only opportunity to travel abroad. I don't know what I'll do when I get back, but I'm leaving for Mexico."

As she emits these words her chin starts to tremble, "If you leave then you can forget about us. I am not waiting for you to 'find yourself' in Mexico. We're through."

Ride

The Jimi Hendrix lyrics, "Well dig, I'm going way down south, way down to Mexico way," echo in my mind as I wake up to the fact that I am in a bus traveling to Cuernavaca Mexico. I feel as if I've returned to a familiar land that I'd forgotten a long time ago. My past makes shadows in my mind, law school, expectation of my love, hopes of my family, my own indecision, and now the bus. Looking out the dew-fogged window I survey the landscape around me. Policemen with their whistles move traffic like great schools of angry metal fish. Buildings half constructed with metal rods thrusting out the side of the cement.

"Quieres coca o café" the words of the bus maid bring me back from me dreams.

"Quiero café gracias." I like this part of Mexico. The buses treat you well, like you're flying. So many things are different yet the same here, if that makes any sense. I'm going to have plenty of time to sort out whatever it is I have on my mind.

For now I sit back and close my eyes, proud I am in Mexico to prove to myself I can do something other than school work.

After an uneventful bus ride I arrive in Cuernavaca, the city of eternal spring. With the temperature hovering near seventy degrees Fahrenheit at eight on a September morning, I understand where the city got its nickname. I step out of the bus, grab my suitcase and roll it across the asphalt to the gray stone tile that lines the inside of the Casino of the Jungle bus stop. I walk through the terminal and over to a cabby with coffee colored skin bulging out of his button-down shirt and ask the price for a ride to Condominium Fresno. He tells me its thirty-five pesos. That's about three dollars and fifty cents. I agree and hop into the front seat while the driver loads my suitcase into the trunk.

We say nothing as the cabby motors along the foreign city street in a beat up VW bug. When I arrive at Condominium Fresno number five, a brick house covered in stucco, the man motions with his thick finger my destination and puts his palm up for the payment. I drop the pesos into his hand and he throws the target-looking coins with their golden circumference and silver middle into the ashtray where he stores his metallic fares.

A woman with a blue dress and shawl thrown across her shoulders greets me. Her name is Carmen, about forty five years old and still pretty, although in her youth she was radiant, the worries of her family and carving a life out of the vibrant city have put lines around her lips and eyes. She helps me with my backpack and I grab the large suitcase from the back of the cab. The cabby motors off. We go inside the sturdy house decorated with shellacked blue suns and eat breakfast.

Quickly, I find myself in bed at the end of the day. My plans run silently through my head, "Why was it so important for me to come down here? One year ago I just wanted to get a regular job or continue with school and move back home. But I just couldn't rest, there was this irritating feeling deep in my chest that

I had to travel to Mexico. It was a throbbing pull like looking at bikini-clad Luna on the beach. Have I made the right decision? Yes, I know I have made the right decision and now I must forget about her and move on with my life. Like she said, we are through."

The weeks pass. I get accustomed to the rhythm of Mexican life. Rising at 6:00 a.m. I eat a breakfast of quesadillas, yogurt, and orange juice with Carmen. Then, dodging traffic, I hurry to a turnabout called La Luna and catch a bus to Centro de Idiomas, where I teach English everyday. The streets are full of energy, and people walk on the cement curbs. Sexy women prance with their hips making small circles. Exhaust lifts from the cars and stings the lungs. The shrieking horns make my blood boil.

It is not possible to rest in this environment. When I give the bus driver his pesos; it's necessary to say where I am going because the bus driver always quickly counts out the change, depending on the destination. I sit in a seat next to an old man. The hands of the old one are wrinkled and colored like the earth. How many years have those hands worked the ground?

A lady enters the bus selling sweets and peanuts screeching in a loud, fast voice. She sells on about 400 buses a day; if only two people on each bus buy her candies, it's a good day. I motion to her and buy a bag of Japanese peanuts, munching on them spilling the crumbs onto the floor.

With a grumble and a roar the bus motors off and the city passes before my eyes. Spanish signs on the side of a yellow wall say things like two for one and Pan Paloma. The sound of the motor is full and vibrates the bus, while techno bounces off the passengers. It's the same music that plays on Saturday nights at a popular night club called Carlos N Charlie's. Some of the people on the bus look at me strangely. I can guess that they're thinking, "What's a white boy doing here in a Mexican bus?" The movement of this country is so different. I smile to myself, looking up.

Dancing

In the past few weeks of working, coming home, and eating with Carmen and her son, Erik, they form an easy friendship with me. Vulker, Carmen's younger son, lives an hour away in Mexico City at a military school, but with the fun weekend nights at Carlos N Charlie's we make a connection. There is nothing like drinking beer to cement friendship.

Going to places by myself is not on the agenda because I don't know the countryside and am nervous to venture out of Cuernavaca alone. My host brothers and their cousin Marcos enjoy a new addition to their trio and I am happy to accompany them on weekend excursions. It seems to be a familiar thread throughout my journey that people include me in all areas of their lives.

After class on Friday, the three of them drop by in a blue sedan and drive us to Acapulco.

Erik, Vulker, Marcos, and I walk beneath the bronze fountain of Diana with her bow pulled taught and athletic rump reflecting in the pool below. The hot air blows between the cars with a mixed smell of the ocean and alcohol. It's like Del Playa, a popular party street at the University of California Santa Barbara, on steroids. I feel my testosterone and instincts pull all around me. Wanting more and more, the hot neon lights flash on and off yelling to the crowd: "Com Here!" "Girls!" "Tequilla!" "Bungee!" Excitement!" "SEX!" The air flows over my shoulders and waist bringing this entire aura with it.

People wearing flashy clothes stand in a long line in front of the club, trying desperately to appear like Ricky Martin or Shakira. Some, remarkably, do have a resemblance. I stand comfortable as myself. In every group there is always the "coolest," someone smooth and slick who gets the women and influences men. In my group, Marcos is that man. With his hair black and slick, pants and shirt cleanly lining his body, he walks up to the bouncer and talks in undertones. The bouncer smirks and nods. The whole group passes into the club as an anxious line of people give us jealous stares.

Despite the looks, Marcos winks at a blonde with blue eyeliner. Lights illuminate the club, making it look like an enormous castle, complete with ivy scaling up both towers. Tiki torches burn along a bridge that leads to an enormous door into the club. The place bounces with people, lights, smoke, alcohol, and sweat mixing into one scent that sticks to skin and clothes. At the bar I quickly take down two tequila shots that burn their way to my empty stomach.

We sit in a corner. Vulker, goes for more beers. The beers in this place are cold and big, two bottles of Corona in each oversized mug. I feel slightly uneasy in this foreign place, so I look over every new customer and try to figure whether they're friendly or one to be avoided.

I feel a needed tranquility, sitting in a bar with my buddies, drinking brews together and looking at girls. The beat of the music draws people to dance; strong men, their hair slicked back, and beautiful women in multicolored blouses hold each other in a grinding sway with arms tight around the back. Lights of the disco ball blink off and on while my thoughts and mind go to a place of obscurity.

Women and music form a place called *Calaboso*, where lust dissolves into a soup that drips into the crowd's veins. Everyone, together on the floor, dance like a giant animal, different parts moving with the rhythm. The creature can feel the musical waves the DJ is mixing while it all washes into the gut of this beast. Four friends laugh and feel what it is like to be young, strong, and dance in a place of obscurity; while women with blood-red lips and coffee skin hold us late into the night.

Friends

Groggy from last night, we get up in the afternoon and travel to meet a friend of the family in a pueblo far away from Acapulco. I have never met this friend before, but when I am with these three the red carpet gets rolled out for us. Erik tells me that Santos, the friend in the pueblo, has a wife who makes excellent fish soup. Hearing this makes me smile because with my dull headache, soup sounds delicious. Whenever I am not feeling well I like to eat soup, something about the heat going down into my stomach and the steam make me feel better.

Although he should not drive, Marcos volunteers to nurse his hang over while guiding the car over the road.

I dose between dreaming and waking, a gentle rain washes the dirt away outside the window. A dream takes me back to California, with eight foot green and purple psychedelic waves crashing on my head. I wake up in Mexico and remnants of the dream echo in my skull.

The soothing sound of rain washes me clean of the tequila and Corona from the night before. Souls can travel to any destination during a dream and my spirit gets restless with set locations, be it north or south. Yet, in both countries I know that the tranquility of water can bring me back into the present moment. Overcast gray skies, moist like perspiration on an early morning run, drop water on the cooked earth.

While Marcos drives the small sedan, I gaze upon the green mountains that stretch out adjacent to the road, and watch fields of sugar cane, huge gray cows, and unfinished houses with rebar pointing into the sky pass by the window.

After driving to Santos's house, gifts and warm hugs are exchanged beneath the dryness of the kitchen. "This is your house," Santos and his wife, Socorro, tell me and I know that they mean it. This type of warmth between people embraces me, and is common in this land unlike much of California. They care about others and deeply want their guests to enjoy themselves.

A painting of Santos greets all that enter. He's holding a carving covered with a blanket, and his face looks ten years younger looming large and deep. Santos is the only thing solid in a constantly moving world. His eyes peer out like a brown bear with cubs. One can tell that this man will protect and care for everything within his world.

➤ Erik is right, the warm salty steam from the red fish soup is delicious and reminds me of the ocean brine being swept from under my feet when standing on the seashore. I have weighty eyelids from barely sleeping the night before and take mouthfuls of salty red generosity. This satisfies me and the rain frames it all in a drop that splashes on the ground. As we all drink, the agua ardiente slowly takes over my bloodstream and it calms my reflexes putting me in an enjoyable buzz.

Santos gives me a personal tour and explains that he is a successful art restorer and refurbishes archeological artifacts. The house is situated beside a gray and blue stream now hidden behind green brush and trees fertilized with hot humid weather and fecund earth. As water moves over rocks below, the creek fills our abode with a comforting sound. The house looks like part of the jungle; with aged wood trim and red bricks around the base in a solid conformation. Rain-worn shingles look very sturdy despite the wear and peppering of the storm. Santos has restored several artifacts that decorate the abode. A stone statue with a pointed Mayan nose stares out from centuries ago, while windows let beams of light through the room to dance on the back of a whitened stained glass Pegasus.

Santos invites all four of us to stay for Christmas and I revel in the feeling of community. The whole neighborhood walks from house to house singing and asking for a place to stay for the night. Reenacting the struggles of Mary and Joseph to find a safe place to sleep, every person holds a candle and sings the song printed on the back of the candle box.

Finally, the people predestined to hold the posada open their doors and bring out the pinatas. Delicious tamales and tacos dorados are quickly devoured. I inhale the sweet tamales with green corn that mix well with hot chocolate atole. The atole has bits of oatmeal inside to give the chocolate a thick consistency that slides down my throat.

People sit around chatting about nothing in particular, just to talk and have fun. I talk to my next door neighbor, a generous lady who always has a smile on her face. She is sixty years old but her eyes have a younger sparkle. They bring out pinatas filled with small fruit, mandarin oranges, sugar cane, peanuts, and candies. I help lift and lower the pinata to prevent anyone from getting a good smack. Erik swings wildly clipping my foot hanging lazily below the wall, and causes an eruption of laughs and shouts, "Hit the pinata, not your friend."

Finally a small child wacks the pinata for all its worth, spilling the goodies everywhere. Adults and children scatter to collect their treats. My Mexican brothers, the Santos family, Marcos, neighbors and I all laugh and smile with the guitars in the music.

Walking

The next holiday that everyone talks about, Dia Mexicana, is finally here. During this festival, the whole town of Zacualpan comes into the street to watch the floats.

Music of the Chinelos bounces around in my head and I dance with the crowd among the colorful floats. The most beautiful is a red and purple dragon. People beneath the papier mache dragon hold wooden poles and sway with the music to make the dragon breath and swarm in between the narrow street filled with parade watchers. Teenagers dance hand in hand in the back of the line, leaping and skipping in a circle to the shrieking blast of the trumpet and the deep thud of the drum.

In front of the line, citizens reenact the Bible and words of scripture live in the village tradition and ceremony. Pure and beautiful, a fifteen year old girl portrays La Virgen de Guadalupe and forces me to make a double take to reassure myself I am not in the presence of the Great Mother herself.

A live St. Michael protects the gates of heaven from a heaving Satan, his green scaly tail threatening the crowd. Parade people continue to dance along the cobblestone village streets. Onlookers stand outside their multicolored painted metal doors, watching. Most have a blank looking expression on their sun darkened faces. Yet, even on the oldest wrinkled face there is a sense of pride and accomplishment beneath the black eyes; a look that is not found anywhere except in small villages where it is the community that brings on the highest satisfactions in life. All the while, grinning grandmas bounce babies on the knee and clap to the music, 1,2,3,4, Hey, and the baby giggles with delight. The trumpets continue to sing.

Treasure

Santos's family has shown me the wonder of village life and true hospitality, as I near the end of my time in Zacualpan there is one thing I've yet to do and that is climb to the top of a nearby mountain.

The only thing I want is to be on the top of the mountain. They say there is magic in her. It is an extraordinary day for hiking. The air is soft like a spring day, not heavy like winter skies and there are small clouds that give shade. My legs feel strong and I have but one thought: to get to the top of the mountain. I try to walk without breathing heavily, using normal steps. All is well until the mountain turns almost perpendicular into the treetops, and my steps become weighted with work. My lungs take deep breaths to bring my body to the top of the mountain. My heart pumps quickly, blood moves rapidly inside my veins and I can feel my life current inside. Blood palpitates inside my hands, and when I stop to rest I hear my heart below my throat making scratching sounds. After a while of feeling the difficulties of the hike, my body adapts and I start a strong rhythm to walk up the mountain. Rhythm helps bring me and the mountain into balance while the mountain allows me to climb. The reward is a marvelous view from Tepozteco.

Returning to the village, I take a less strenuous path along a creek with Santos's family. Thick trees cover the ground of the mountain and their roots reach into the ground drinking deep of the cold spring water. At the foot of the mountain the stream flows into a flat marshland, forming a small lake. The family spreads out a blanket to eat beef tacos and spicy salsa beneath the afternoon sun. After lunch I wander to the edge of the lake. Sleepy from the food, all the blood seeps out of my head and into my stomach. As the food digests, I lazily watch some fish at the edge of the lake. I imagine what being a fish is like.

Fish love to swim with their friends in a lake surrounded by green grass and guarded by a mountain. The palms grow freely toward a sky that is almost always blue. Most lakes have a bottom of mud, and when the fish swim their tails throw up debris and muck throughout the water. Not here, in this lake, multicolored pebbles allow creatures in the lake to see very well because the little stones are not easily disturbed. The fish thanked destiny for putting them in a wonderful lake. They spend many hours playing in the bottom of the lake. They have races around the old roots that stick out of the bottom of the mud. Many trees once grew in the lake, but when the water grew to a high level the trees drowned and left only their roots in place.

A day of tranquility ends for the fish when I enter the lake and try to catch them. The fish hide to escape my quick hands. Disappointed I throw my head out of the water and take a deep breath. I'm so enthralled watching the fish that I decide to join them. Yet, without a spear to hunt them, I will never catch a fish. In the end the fish win. I return to the picnic empty-handed.

Sadly, my time in the small village comes to an end. I say my good-byes to the Santos family. My three friends and I have plans to visit Guanajuato, and we pile into the sedan.

I sleep most of the time on the highway, tired from all the bouncing festivals and high mountaintops. After hours of traveling I feel the car slow down during my slumber. With sleep stuck to my eyes, I stretch and yawn while stiffly exiting the car. My three friends are already at the stands buying cookies and snacks for the rest of the trip. I head to the bathroom limping from the full bottle of water I drank at the beginning of our ride. When I get out of the facilities my host brother Erik watches me, and munches on popcorn with a smirk on his face.

"Its about time, lets go." Erik throws down the empty paper sack of popcorn while I get in and the car pulls out of the rest area.

We travel many more hours and finally pass by the enormous statue that keeps guard of the entrance to Guanajuato. Earth-colored light orange bricks shape the giant's form. The titan stands guard on his city with a massive torch and rippling abdominal muscles. Vistas of any city are impressive, but the churches of the valley stand out, tall steeples and bells adorn the various religious buildings below. They are about five kilometers away, but their grandiose size makes it seem like I can pluck the steeples out of the landscape. The enormous valley and the different colored houses in the bright sunlight make a multicolored mosaic of the city below, green, yellow, red, and brown all mixing into the landscape. On the outskirts, trees and one or two houses intersperse the green fields. Once revolutionary, the city now hums tranquility.

In this city, Mexicans took their independence under the leadership of Padre Miguel Hidalgo. One man stormed the enormous walls of the city government building with a flat heavy boulder on his back. The guards tried and tried to shoot him, but the rock was bulletproof. He got close enough to the front gate to blow it to pieces with dynamite. He gave his life and became a hero. Now the city building is a museum with pictures and history of Mexican life, yet on the inside of the walls are murals of the Mexican struggle. The expressions on the faces and the vivid colors help visitors feel this part of history.

As we pull up to the museum, the sun bakes the parking lot with a vengeance. "Mummies of Guanajuato," the museum entrance proclaims. Outside the building, trinket hawkers show their goods; Mexican finger traps, caramel replicas of mummies, and knives of different sorts. There are even dirty key chains that every nine-year-old school boy would get a kick out of—men and women doing it in different positions, complete with movable parts. When I arrived in Mexico, the clamor of street hawkers made me nervous, but now that I'm accustomed to it, I enjoy seeing what they have to offer. Even the most intelligent Mexican professionals, like lawyers and dentists, work two jobs to supplement their income. I understand the hustle of the street sellers because everyone in this country must hustle and struggle to make a life.

Entering the hallways of the museum, I see case after case of preserved corpses. Due to the soil contents and the heat in Guanajuato, buried people become mummies. Men and women of different sizes, with their hair intact, all have disturbing looks on their faces. The process of drying has pulled the lips and eyelids half shut resembling a squinty eyed grimace. It makes sense, no one is ecstatic about being dead. A grimace is appropriate.

As a tourist attraction, some of the mummies have been on display for 100 years, and their clothes remain intact. Strange to see the clothes still present on the bodies; pants, socks, dresses, all clinging to the dried up jerky skin. A preserved fetus, the smallest mummy in the world rounds out the collection of dead.

Upon leaving the salon I feel disturbed and a little sad. This is my fate; to live out my days only to end up dried and lifeless after a handful of years. Ironically, every form of life on earth has the same destiny—to spend some time here and die. Perhaps I can contribute before I go. At least there will be memories of love before I become a piece of jerky. Better yet, I will tell my relatives to burn my body and throw the ashes into the Pacific Ocean or scatter them on top of Coche Peak.

Insight

Next stop on our vagabond journey is Queretaro, a few hundred miles from the soil-preserved corpses. Erik has a relative in the city that loves motorcycles and enjoys spreading the excitement of this sport.

The aunt makes a dinner of roasted chicken and the uncle wanders out to the garage after he eats his fill. I follow him in anticipation of his speedy hobby. The death of the last adventure has me craving life, and energy surges through my veins as Erik's uncle revs the motorcycle. Uncle Santiago, a daredevil in disguise of a normal family man, maneuvers the bike. I sit behind Santiago on the noisy beast watching the ground race beneath the wheels and feel the wind beating on my face. Once at the top of the mountain, during the end of the ride, I can see the arches of Queretaro, built to support an aqueduct 300 years ago. Spotlights illuminate the pillars against the ebony night sky, making them look like a monument to a Roman god. The ancient aqueduct stretches four kilometers, and takes the imagination on a ride along its well-lit pathway.

The next day I take a stroll through the city with my host family. Streets are exceedingly clean; fountains, large and bronze, are the image of Europe three centuries years ago. They pour out cool crisp water into the center of the bowl and pigeons come to drink. Poseidon, with powerful muscles and a shimmering metal trident, emerges from the surface of the sea as water splashes on his back. Horses and warriors march in the water, splashing the liquid everywhere. A solid metal ball with water falling all over the surface, appears to be spinning in mid air and fascinates children the most.

The walkways are enormous. The cobblestone roads give the impression of carriages and long flowing dresses. When women walk on them with high heels, the clogging sound resonates in the street. The openness of the different centers provide a relaxed atmosphere that all enjoy. Husbands and wives stroll hand and hand, sometimes with little children leading the way. They giggle and laugh with each step and continue in their quest to explore the different parts of the center. Other children, the more rambunctious ones, fight with siblings in front of the parents. They contribute something more true-to-life with their whine and cry that echos on the cobblestone roads. The balloon vendor knows this whine quite well. He depends on it to sell his balloons. "Mami, papi I want a balloon, please get me a balloon." He shakes his rattle balloon and attracts the small children.

The trees around the square are beautifully trimmed in long interspersed rectangles. They show a bright green light that sparkles in front of the enormous public buildings. Flowers burst in different colors, red, yellow, and blue, in the planters that sprout the shimmering green trees. The waiters in front of various restaurants smile and invite strollers to enter and enjoy a meal. The men have suits and a white shiny smile while the women have tight gray stockings on shapely legs. These beauties in trimmed skirts are hard to turn down.

The restaurants preserve a colonial ambiance. This beautiful colonial setting, frequented by the rich of Mexico, does come at a cost. Behind the luxurious gates and block walls in the corner and sometimes in the front are uniformed armed guards. Some of them carry machine guns slung across their shoulder and others wear only a handgun at the hip. They look friendly enough, but one could only imagine their attitude if thieves or robbers tried to harm the castles they protect.

Inside these buildings from the past are displays of craft paintings and architecture that inspire the imagination, there is a miniature model of Queretaro at night, amazingly life-like. I can see the different shades of yellow lighting, while the mountains shine gray in the moonlight and above them is a dark blue night sky. The town lamps sparkle and illustrate the different dimensions of the city as the lights rise and fall on the inclines and the valleys of the landscape.

It's only a model, but my imagination is sparked by the intricacy of the artist's plan. On the wall hangs a painting of Michael the Archangel. With his sword and battle armor, his skin jumps off the canvas as he fights evil.

In the center courtyard, natural sunlight seeps through a high cloth. The aroma of the fountain, surrounded by plants, makes for a sensual treat. The waiters and greeters in suits still smile and beckon as we leave.

We walk as a group; the aunts, uncles, cousins, adults, and children. I enjoy being close to them and passing time with my adopted family. It strikes me as strange that I had visited this place and stayed with these people before. I realize that I have not thought about Luna for months, as Mexico has cleansed her from my mind; when a friendly deja vu grips me. Eight months ago Luna said in a dream I had, "Make sure you are thankful for all they do, and please speak Spanish."

Place

My time in Mexico comes to an end and I must return to the United States. I can tell from my last call home that my mother wants me to get back by Mother's Day, but doesn't have much hope I will. With my money slowly running out and a new boss at the language school, I decide it's time to book a flight back home.

I kiss my host mother Carmen goodbye and climb into the airport cab quickly, to avoid tears that I feel welling up behind my eyelids.

Stars and stripes float vividly in the distance across from Tijuana. Above me the eagle screeches in the breeze, while sitting on top of a cactus. Two cultures, two ways of living, have become a part of me. After eight months in the south I feel like I have tequila flowing through my heart. A country has adopted me. With these friendly people hawking for cash in the streets, I am imbued by the culture's openness. My host family took me in, shared quesadillas and orange juice with me in the morning and served up hot carne asadas on Saturday afternoons. I feel like a brother. Coming out of my private thoughts I chat in Spanish with a husband and wife.

"This line sure is long," I open the conversation.

"Yes it is long, but it is better than driving across. We'd rather cross on foot anytime."

"Where are you from?" I ask the couple.

"We're from Morelos." They say with blank faces.

"Seriously, I just spent eight months in Morelos. I was teaching English in Cuernavaca."

"That's great! Morelos is wonderful, there are a lot of things to do there. Did you climb the Tepozteco?"

"Yeah , I did! It was a rush getting to the top and seeing the whole valley. People there believe in the natural powers of the mountain. One man was meditating in the middle of the temple with beads around his neck and flowing white clothing on his body."

"Finally the line is moving. Maybe we will get through some time today. It seems you had a great time, and you speak Spanish well." The husband and wife shake my hand, giving me a touching compliment, as the line begins to move.

After three hours I finally get to the front of the line. The border patrol officer stares at me blankly in his blue uniform. In America everyone is a mixture of races, cultures, and attitudes, in Mexico there is more homogeneity in the faces around me. The officer has Asian features molded into his face, yet his tone and direct speech portray truly American communication and seriousness. "Citizenship" he mumbles.

"American" I state confidently.

"How long were you in Mexico?" He questions.

"Eight months." I reply even though I have nothing to fear my stomach twists and turns under his glare.

"Are you carrying any food, fruits, vegetables, or animals?" This is his next question.

"No." I'm hoping he doesn't go through my bag and find the coffee and chocolate I want to bring back to my grandfather.

"What were you doing in Mexico?' He's trying to get me to say something wrong if I'm up to no good.

"I was teaching English in Cuernavaca." I reply.

"Oh, that's cool! My sister is a teacher. I bet you speak Spanish pretty good now?" He livens up.

"Yeah I do." I smile.

"Welcome back." He finally lets me through the turnstile.

I cross through the boarder and walk to the Red Line Metro that will take me to Amtrack in San Diego. At the train station I will be able to take the Surfliner all the way up the coast to my home in Santa

Maria. My mom will be surprised when I arrive home the day before Mother's Day.

When I'm dropped off at the bus station in Santa Maria, it's already dark. The night sky is deep black against the white stars. The moon is full, and with the mist in the air it makes an enormous halo of water droplets. Since my house is close to the station, I walk home loaded down with my rolling suitcase and bag full of presents for my family.

As I come up the front porch of my parent's house, the wheels of my dark suitcase echo in the neighborhood like a skateboard hitting cracks in the cement. I ring the doorbell and my father gets up to answer, with his T-shirt glowing behind the stained glass picture fitted into the door.

"Who is it?" He yells gruffly.

"Its me, Tony." I say, caught off guard by my father's angry voice.

"Who?" He questions less aggressive.

"Your son." I shout.

"Anthony? Its you? What are you doing here?" He swings the door open. By this time my mom stands behind my father in her bathrobe. "I don't believe it, I'm so glad you're home." My father shakes his head in pleased disbelief. I give my father a hug and hold on tight, I can smell the sleep on his T-shirt. My mom pulls me in and kisses me on the cheek.

"You grew a beard." She exclaims. I grin happily as she continues, "I was just saying my prayers and drifting off to sleep, I asked God to take care of you in Mexico and then I heard something like a skateboard outside the door. You didn't tell us you were coming home."

"I wanted to surprise you for Mother's Day." I say, laughing softly.

We go into the kitchen and drink hot green tea while I tell them of my voyage. My parents are excited to see me in person. I show them all the gifts that I brought back from Mexico. We all glow from being reunited, despite my exhaustion from the trip. During a silence from conversation, I stare at the table and wonder what I'm going to do with myself now.

Passion

College graduate, world traveler, bilingual, so many credits to tack onto my resume, yet no job.

The weekly drives to Los Angeles are wearing down on me, and every job fair is the same thing. Job fair interviewer, "What have you done for the last year?"

"I taught English in Mexico."

Job fair interviewer, "Well I've never heard of anyone traveling after college. You don't have the job experience we are looking for. We'll call you when a position opens up."

They're all small thinkers. I know traveling was a good idea; I grew more than anyone will ever know. Regardless, here I am without any prospects.

As I return home on the 101 through the San Fernando Valley, these thoughts pass under my mind like the asphalt underneath my wheels. All the different colored cars are racing toward the same direction. My brown Saturn is caught up amidst the school of cars swimming between two large mountain ranges under a light yellow haze. The highway presses under me and I'm squashed in my vehicle between the blurring heat, black racing pavement, and thoughts of unemployment. I drive on, head pointed straight, staring off into the distance, hard LA rap bouncing off my skull keeping me awake.

After three hours convincing interviewers I was the best, I want to leave Los Angles and all its judgements behind. I can see the top of the dusty brown mountains signaling the end of the basin. Once I cross those mountains I'll be out of the big city. Crossing over, I can feel the gloom lift off of me, as traffic diminishes. Slowly the Pacific Ocean seeps into view, stretching out forever.

Back at home, a glass stares back at me, blue green, and sections of sun kissed water sparkle like newly minted coins. "What do I do? I'll never find a job here." I complain. My mom responds with a shake of her head and smiling eyes.

"You always wanted to live in your hometown. There must be something you can do." Silence. Then she suggests, "What about going down to the school district and signing up to substitute teach?"

I nod and gulp down a glass of water and finish my tuna sandwich. "Why didn't I think of that before?" I ask myself. I head out the door, go to the Office of Education, and pick up the paper work and an application. An hour later sitting at the desk with ten pieces of paper I carefully type out the application. First impressions are everything so it must be professionally done. The stapled pages represent me and I want to look good. After revisions, when I feel the application is perfect, I exhale forcefully.

When I get to the office the following day, my stomach is jumpy like a can of fresh 7UP quickly fizzing inside. The application feels heavy. I scrutinize it one last time to be sure there are no errors.

I look around for the human resources department. It's up the stairs. With rookie enthusiasm, I bound up the stairs and walk through the doorway. "Hello, I have an appointment with the personnel secretary at 1:00." I state slightly out of breath.

"Yes, take a seat. I'm the personnel secretary." A woman in a navy blue dress with a white line down the side extends her hand toward a chair. Taking my seat, I place my folder with extra resumes on my lap and wait while she examines my application. She takes a long time to go through it, makes several "Hmms," and clicks with her tongue as she reads. As I watch her read I'm thrown off guard. People usually don't look through applications this thoroughly on the first meeting. Finally she speaks. "Why, Mr. Montani?"

"Excuse me?"

"Why did you go to Mexico? And, why didn't you come to our office earlier this summer? No science people we interview can speak Spanish, and 95% of our student population is Latino. You fit the bill. Would you like to work for us?"

A word quickly comes to my tongue. This word started out lost and made a journey across half a continent. Now it is here, "Yes."

Niche

On the first day of class, I sit at the desk bouncing my knee and fidgeting with a yellow #2 pencil. The regular teacher left excellent lesson plans and everything is in place, but it's difficult to tell what's going to happen. A class of thirty energetic seventh graders could get out of control quickly. I imagine thirty students running around the room with more energy than a bus-crammed street in Cuernavaca. The bell rings, in come the students.

While I hand out worksheets filled with black typing, the students are surprisingly quiet. They smile and giggle when I ask them if they need any help. I suppose most substitutes sit at the desk and don't mingle around the room, but I think good teachers work the room and get close to the students; with a performance presence like Wayne Newton. One student is gazing off into space and tapping the side of the metal desk with his ring.

"What's up, how is that problem going?" I ask.

"He doesn't speak English." Two female students give up his secret quickly.

I ask, "Como puedo ayudar?" That means, "How can I help?"

"You speak Spanish!" Several astonished students gasp in unison.

"Claro." I nod my head like I always have.

"That is good to know because..."one of the girls confesses. "Not many of the substitutes know Spanish."

Once again I get Cuernavaca bus stares from the students who are thinking, "What's this guy doing speaking Spanish." The confused student is looking directly at me. Instead of a deer in the headlights look, he has hopefulness about him.

"You need to divide by two and recheck your answer." I counsel him. He quickly scribbles something in the margin and turns back grinning. "Ya, ya entiendo." Alright, alright, I understand.

That night I lie in bed and thoughts chatter through my mind. Soothing me to sleep the dark room closes over me like a curtain coming down at the end of a play. I reach a turning point in my life and realize I found my niche today in the classroom. Something feels right about the whole situation deep inside my bones, although it's only the first day. Why go to Mexico? Now beginning a life in my hometown I know why. After my journey through the unknown I can embrace the known.

About the Author

Mike Muscio teaches 8th grade Science in Santa Maria, California. He enjoys the Central Coast immensely with its rugged mountains and wide ocean views. At the University of California Santa Barbara, he earned a Bachelor of Science in Pharmacology.

Quick Order Form

Online Orders http://mysite.verizon.net/res7zqu8/

Postal Orders

PO Box 2933

Santa Maria CA 93457

Please send ___ copies of Paisano's Passion.

I understand that I may return the book for a full

refund – for any reason, no questions asked.

Please send the books to

Name: _____

Address: _____

City: _____ State: ____ Zip: _____ Telephone:

email: _____

Sales tax: Please add 7.75 % for products shipped to

California addresses.

Shipping by air: US $4 for the first book and $2 for

each additional book.

Payment: Cheque or Credit Card:

Visa Mastercard Optima AMEX Discover Card

Number: _____

Name on Card: _____

Exp. Date: ___ / ____

Quick Order Form

Online Orders http://mysite.verizon.net/res7zqu8/

Postal Orders

PO Box 2933

Santa Maria CA 93457

Please send ___ copies of Paisano's Passion.

I understand that I may return the book for a full

refund – for any reason, no questions asked.

Please send the books to

Name: _____

Address: _____

City: _____ State: ____ Zip: _____ Telephone:

email: _____

Sales tax: Please add 7.75 % for products shipped to

California addresses.

Shipping by air: US $4 for the first book and $2 for

each additional book.

Payment: Cheque or Credit Card:

Visa Mastercard Optima AMEX Discover Card

Number: _____

Name on Card: _____

Exp. Date: ___ / ___